ZIP! POP! HOP!
AND OTHER FUN WORDS TO SAY

By Michaela Muntean
Illustrated by David Prebenna

SO-CCJ-339

Featuring Jim Henson's Sesame Street Muppets

 A GOLDEN BOOK • NEW YORK

Published by Golden Books Publishing Company, Inc.,
in conjunction with Children's Television Workshop

A portion of the money you pay for this book goes to Children's Television Workshop. It is put right back into SESAME STREET and other CTW educational projects. Thanks for helping!

Elmo likes fun words. Would you like to say some fun words with Elmo?

Say zipper. Now stretch it out:

Z–Z–Z–Z–Z–ZIPPER.

Words with *z*'s make your mouth feel fizzy.

Look! Here are four more fun words:
Pickle! Pizza! Pumpkin! Popcorn!

POP-POP-POP-POPCORN!

Watch Elmo play hopscotch. **HOP, HOP, HOP!**

Slimey can't hop. He wiggles.
Do you think worms play **wigglescotch?**

Elmo is getting a fur cut. *SNIP, SNIP,* **CLIP, CLIP.**

Zoe can roar like a lion. R-R-R-R-R-**ROAR!**

Elmo can growl like a bear. GR-R-R-R-**OWL!**

Elmo and Zoe walk in the crinkly fall leaves.
CRUNCH! CRUNCH! CRUNCH!

Listen to the bee buzz, Zoe!
Buzz-z-z-z-z.

Thump, thump, thump is the sound of a
bouncing ball.

PLOP! Zoe and Elmo play in a mud puddle. Squishy-squashy mud feels great!

SPLISH, SPLASH.
Soon Elmo will be squeaky clean.

The water swirls down the drain.
GURGLE, GURGLE, GLUG, GLUG!

Elmo's favorite pajamas have **squiggly** lines.

At bedtime Elmo's daddy sings a song.
Sometimes Elmo hums along.

Hmm-mmm-mmm-mmm...

Elmo's blanket is warm and snuggly.
The clock goes
TICK-TOCK, TICK-TOCK.

RAT-A-TAT, RAT-A-TAT.
The rain beats against the windowpane.
WOO-OO-OO-OO.
The wind rushes through the trees.

Nighty-night, sleep tight!